CHILLERS

The Dinn

D1102625

TESSA POTTER

Illustrated by
KAREN DONNELLY

PUFFIN BOOKS

CHILLERS

The Blob Tessa Potter and Peter Cottrill
Clive and the Missing Finger Sarah Garland
The Day Matt Sold Great-grandma Eleanor Allen and Jane Cope
The Dinner Lady Tessa Potter and Karen Donnelly
Ghost from the Sea Eleanor Allen and Leanne Franson
Hide and Shriek! Paul Dowling
Jimmy Woods and the Big Bad Wolf Mick Gowar and Barry Wilkinson
Madam Sizzers Sarah Garland
The Real Porky Philips Mark Haddon
Sarah Scarer Sally Christie and Claudio Muñoz
Spooked Philip Wooderson and Jane Cope
Wilf and the Black Hole Hiawyn Oram and Dee Shulman

PUFFIN BOOKS

Published by the Penguin Group
Penguin Books Ltd, 27 Wrights Lane, London W8 5TZ, England
Penguin Books USA Inc., 375 Hudson Street, New York, New York 10014, USA
Penguin Books Australia Ltd, Ringwood, Victoria, Australia
Penguin Books Canada Ltd, 10 Alcorn Avenue, Toronto, Ontario, Canada M4V 3B2
Penguin Books (NZ) Ltd, 182–190 Wairau Road, Auckland 10, New Zealand

Penguin Books Ltd, Registered Offices: Harmondsworth, Middlesex, England

First published by A&C Black (Publishers) Ltd 1995
Published in Puffin Books 1997
3 5 7 9 10 8 6 4 2

Filmset in Meridien

Made and printed in England by William Clowes Ltd, Beccles and London

Chapter One
The Flash

Everyone thinks dinner ladies are kind people who like working with children. Maybe most of them are, but the one in our school was no ordinary dinner lady. At least I don't think she was.

It all started the day we had extra maths with Miss Swan. I'd been looking out of the window, thinking when...

Jessica! Will you GET ON!

there was a terrific flash of light in the playground.

The flash was so bright it hurt my eyes. Nobody else saw it, they all had their heads in their books. I practically jumped out of my seat.

"In the playground," I stammered, "a big flash, something's landed there."

"Jessica!" said Miss Swan.

"Probably just a meteorite," said Stacey Smith, "or a bit of a plane dropping off."

Everybody charged to the window.

"But Miss, I did, I really did see something – just for a second. It was a bright white light."

"There's nothing out there," said Stacey who was closest to the window. "There's nothing on the ground. If a meteorite had burnt up on impact it would have left some kind of mark."

Stacey knew everything. It was very tedious.

"Thank you Stacey. Now would you all please get on," said Miss Swan. "And Jessica if you don't get your work finished you'll stay in at break."

I raced through the last sums. I wanted to get out there. I had to see for myself. I felt strange – sort of cold inside. My heart was beating fast. My hands were shaking. I couldn't hold the pencil to do the lines straight. Something had happened, I knew it. I didn't know then what it was. But that's when it started. That bright flash of light was the beginning of it all.

I went outside with Josie at break. She was my best friend. We stood outside the classroom window whilst I tried to work out exactly where the flash had been.

There were no unusual marks on the ground. But when I knelt down and felt around with my hands, a small patch of the concrete seemed incredibly hot.

Josie knelt down. "I can't feel anything."
She looked at me in a strange way.
"Are you sure you're all right Jess?"

I shrugged. "I don't know. I do feel a bit
cold and shivery and my head's killing."
I had to go home at lunch-time.
Miss Swan phoned my mum to say I was
ill and she came for me.

All that happened the same day the new
dinner lady arrived. Josie said
it was just a coincidence,
but I don't think so.

Chapter Two
Just call me Mrs T

To look at, the new dinner lady was like any other dinner lady – although she was a lot younger than our last one. Mrs Blossom had been just like she sounded – kind, with rosy round cheeks. Everyone liked her. We never really knew why she had left so suddenly. They just said she'd been taken ill.

Miss Stoney, the head, was very pleased to get a new dinner lady so quickly. It was only two weeks before the end of term. If they hadn't found one, the teachers would have had to give up their lunch-breaks to look after us.

I was only off school for a day but when I got back, there she was – the new dinner lady, settled in and acting as though she'd been there all her life. She already knew everybody's name. She even knew mine.

She had a big smile
on her face. I nudged
Josie. "Is she always like that –
talking a lot?" And Josie just shrugged.

"Hurry up dears, hurry along please,
there's good children. Make sure your
hands are nice and clean."

I don't know why, I just felt, YUK! She
was all over us and she didn't even know
us yet. I wished Mrs Blossom would come
back. You felt comfortable with her.

11

Even the teachers called the new dinner lady Mrs T. She had some long name that was impossible to pronounce. I found myself staring at Mrs T that first dinner-time. I don't think she noticed, she was so busy smiling and talking.

"Have you seen her eyes?" I said to Josie, who had a mouthful of chips.

"What?" she spluttered.

"Mrs T – her eyes. You know she's always smiling and everything. Well, her eyes don't smile. They're blank and empty – cold and staring like a dead person's."

"Shut up! You're ruining my fish fingers."

Suddenly, Mrs T was standing next to us, telling us to please tidy our plates away nicely. I felt myself shiver. I had that weird cold feeling inside again.

13

I noticed a lot of things about Mrs T that first dinner-time. It was only a small school, so all the juniors and infants played together in the playground. Josie and I were checking the rainfall measurements for Miss Swan.

What's going on over there?

Mrs T had all the infants up at one end of the playground. She'd got them playing a really wild chasing game. It was some kind of tag. They were tearing round and round, and grabbing each other's coats and hair. They were fighting and tripping each other up. A lot of the little ones had fallen over and grazed their knees. They were crying.

I couldn't understand
why Mrs T wasn't getting them to play
nicely, like dinner ladies are supposed to.
Why was she just standing there with a
big grin on her face? It was horrible. But
that wasn't all. Something peculiar was
happening. Mrs T seemed to be changing.

At dinner her red hair had been dull and stringy like straw and her face and legs had been thin and shrivelled-looking. But now, her hair seemed to be shining and glowing. The skin on her face and legs looked tight and stretched, as if she were about to burst out of it. And her nails had grown really long. I know that because when the whistle went, I ran past her and accidentally knocked against her hand. Her nails tore my skin and her hand felt cold and clammy.

By the time Miss Stoney came out to fetch the infants, Mrs T had them all playing quiet singing games. Miss Stoney didn't seem to notice their cut knees and tear-stained faces. All the teachers seemed to think Mrs T was very good, very organised. She was always making them cups of tea. They didn't seem to notice that things got worse and worse.

Chapter Three
Little Things Add Up

That first week, there were
fights and upsets in the
playground every dinner-
time. Best friends began
to quarrel and there was
always someone crying.
I was sure Mrs T was
behind it.

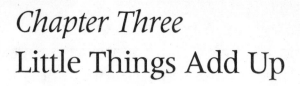

I watched her carefully. It was little things
all the time. She caught Gemma out in
skipping and made it look as though Kelly
had done it. Kelly and Gemma wouldn't
talk to each other for the rest of the day.

The more crying
and upset there was, the
better Mrs T seemed to like it. And after
what she did to Jamie Smith, I decided
there was something really evil about her.

Jamie had only been in the school a few weeks, but everyone really liked him. His best friend was Darren Short. They did everything together. But soon after Mrs T came, all that changed.

One morning, Josie and I got to school early. Jamie was in the playground, hunched up against the wall. We asked him what the matter was, but he just shrugged and kept staring at the ground. He looked small and thin, and he was very pale.

Mrs T came out of the door, looking large and glowing. Lipstick was almost dripping off her lips. She grinned at Jamie.

"Hello Jamie. Down in the dumps again are we? Never mind."
And she moved away towards the gate.

...youth club. Just what's needed. ...keep them out of trouble. HA HA HA HA OH YES. HA HA HA And a disco! Marvellous idea! Oh you ARE wonderful. HA HA HA HAH HA HA HA

We could hear her laughing loudly and chatting with the mothers who were arriving with the little ones. The mothers were all over her. They thought she was wonderful because she had started a youth club in the village. Josie had been to the first club the night before, but I hadn't wanted to go. She said it was great and Mrs T even did a disco.

Jamie followed us into class. He was just standing in the doorway when Simon Bates shoved past him.

Move out of the way Sniffy!

I told Simon to leave him alone, but he just laughed.

He's a misery.

I knew Simon was a bit jealous of Jamie, but I'd never really seen him be horrible like this before. Josie said it had started at the youth club. Jamie had cried when he tripped over Simon's foot and hurt himself badly. Everyone had laughed – even Darren – when Mrs T had called him a:

BIG BABY!

Things weren't any better when Miss Swan came into class. She asked Jamie to speak up when she did the register. Jamie just gulped as though he was trying to hold back tears. I heard Simon whisper:

I watched her at dinner-play. She was organising a game where everybody had to have a partner. She told us all to choose a friend. Darren was next to Jamie, trying to cheer him up. But Mrs T called out:

She took hold of Jamie.

Now, dear, who shall we find to put you with?

But Jamie ran off and refused to play. He stayed by the wall all through dinner-play, staring hard at the ground. I could see he was really upset.

Then Miss Swan came out and blew the whistle and we all had to line up. Simon stuck close to Darren. As they lined up behind Jamie, he whispered:

Jamie thumped Simon and ran into the cloakroom.

Miss Swan looked horrified.

Mrs T turned to us with her big grin, then swung round and walked out of the playground, her high heels clicking. The backs of her legs seemed to be bulging, writhing. Her hair was bright red and trembling in the sun, and swayed from side to side as though it was alive.

I felt very cold and sick. Every day it had been the same. Mrs T arrived looking thin and lifeless, her hair hanging limply, her legs and face shrivelled.

Then by the end of every dinner-play and all the upset, she had changed – changed horribly. She seemed to have swelled up. It was as if in some awful way Mrs T was feeding off our misery. She was thriving on it.

It wasn't just that she liked making us unhappy, she actually needed children's misery to keep her alive, just like ordinary people need food. Come to think of it, I had never actually seen her eat anything!

Suddenly, it all began to fit together. That flash in the playground – that was her beaming down. Mrs T wasn't a *real* person; just some*thing* disguised as one. Something awful from outer space! She wasn't a real dinner lady at all.

I had to talk to someone. But who? Who would believe me?

Chapter Four
The Truth Dawns

I tried to talk to Josie at next play, but she wasn't really interested.

"You're crazy," she said. "I know she's a bit weird and not as nice as Mrs Blossom was, and she's always grinning and upsetting people. But...an alien!"

You're nuts!

And she turned to go.

"Wait, listen." I tried to explain. "If she was a real person, she'd eat food wouldn't she? Human food. Have you ever seen her eat anything at school?"

"She probably has her dinner when she gets home," said Josie.

"She doesn't eat food because she doesn't need it. She's not a human being at all."

"Well, her disco was very good last night, there were even coloured lights."

I don't think she's too bad, really.

I couldn't seem to make Josie understand. I found myself shouting at her.

JOSIE, LISTEN! What about Jamie? Haven't you noticed what she's doing to him?

Josie didn't seem to hear me.

"Jamie's mum tried to spoil things," said Josie. "She wanted to get the disco stopped because she said there ought to be more grown-ups there. She had a big argument with Mrs T about it. Anyway, Mrs T is still going to organise another disco next week, a fancy dress one and then, maybe karaoke.

I was practically screaming now.

LISTEN JOSIE!
I really do think there's something WEIRD about her.

You're the WEIRD one!

"Anyway," she added, "the bell's gone. I'm going inside." She left me just standing there. I felt miserable. Perhaps I *was* going crazy.

I couldn't concentrate during science. My head was hurting and Josie didn't sit next to me as she usually did. I closed my eyes.

I couldn't stop thinking about Mrs T. I could see her thin tongue flicking in and out and those dark blank eyes. She was waiting until feeding time, waiting until dinner-play, so she could feed on our misery!

"It contains three times more mass than the other eight planets put together. It is mostly made of gasses and liquids with a small rocky core…"

I was staring at Stacey. Perhaps *she* would believe me. She was always going on about the possibility of life in other galaxies, and things like that. Even if Josie thought I was crazy or stupid, at least Stacey might understand.

35

Chapter Five
Alien Profile

Next day, I told Stacey everything. She didn't laugh. She looked quite serious – even though she hadn't believed me before about the flash of light.

It was a wet dinner-play. We were in the girls' cloakroom. We should have been in the hall with Mrs T. I began to wish I hadn't asked Josie to come. She kept interrupting.

But Stacey was really serious. "Did you know that hundreds of people have had encounters with extra-terrestial beings? It's all kept quiet though, for security reasons."

You're off your head.

Josie was looking really bored.

"We need to build up a PROFILE," Stacey said. "We need to write down exactly what she's like – any special powers or unusual behaviour."

"Well, she's got very cold hands, clammy and scaly," I said.

"And from what you've said...

1. Doesn't eat human food?

I've put a question mark though. We need more proof.

Now...
Does she go to the toilet?" Stacey asked.

3. Uses the toilet? yes ☐ no ☐

"What do you want to know THAT for?" shrieked Josie. Josie could be really silly sometimes.

"If she doesn't eat, silly, she won't need to go," I said, and turned back to Stacey. "She goes to the staff cloakroom to get her coat. But I don't know what else she does in there!"

"OK, we'll leave that. Now, what else?"

4. Intelligence/ Special powers

"She can change people. She can make them miserable and start acting differently," I said.

39

"You mean like when I was saying to Josie about Mrs T's eyes being like a dead body's, and then she was suddenly right there next to us as though she knew I was talking about her?"

"I'm afraid it's possible. From now on we'll have to try and fool her somehow. She mustn't think we're on to her. We mustn't let her know we're frightened in any way. Try and empty your mind when you're near her. Think about something else, something funny…"

Josie said later it was just the toilet cistern and us being creepy that made her scream. I don't think so.

We looked towards the door. Mrs T was standing there. She was *smiling*! "Come along you three," she said. "You should all be in the hall."

Josie and Stacey darted out like rabbits. I tried to follow, staring hard at the floor.

The others had disappeared.

I swallowed. Think funny, I told myself, like Stacey said. Don't let her know you're scared. I couldn't think of anything funny. I could hardly think at all. My heart was pounding.

I wanted to scream.
I wanted to get out of
there. I wanted to be a
hundred miles away from Mrs T.

"That's good then," she said. "Would you
mind picking up these coats for me dear?
Someone's left them all over the floor. It
doesn't look very tidy, does it?"

When she'd gone, I looked at myself in
the mirror. I was completely white.

Stacey and Josie were waiting for me outside. I collapsed against the wall.

"Are you OK?" asked Stacey anxiously.

"Honestly, I wish I'd gone into the hall in the first place. You nearly got us into trouble," said Josie.

"What are we going to do?" I whispered to Stacey.

Josie ran on ahead of us into the hall.

When we got to the hall, Stacey and I stood for a moment in the doorway. It was very noisy, as usual. Everyone was tearing around, tripping each other up and falling over. Some of the little ones were crying. I could see Jamie. I don't know what he'd done wrong, but Mrs T had made him stand on his own.

Chapter Six
The Head Can't See It

The next morning Stacey and I went to see Miss Stoney. Josie wouldn't come with us, although I asked her to. She just flounced off with Kelly, saying, "I think you've gone really potty, Jessica Brown."

I was going to do the talking but when I tried to explain, it came out all wrong. I couldn't actually say it face to face – not about the flash of light and everything. And about Mrs T practically growing out of her skin each day, even though she never ate any food. I just told Miss Stoney about the little ones getting upset at playtime and how Jamie had changed.

"Well, thank you for your concern," said Miss Stoney. "We all knew Mrs Blossom for so long, I'm sure it may take a bit of time to get used to a new person. But we were very lucky to have Mrs T step in like that at such short notice."

But she's not a person! She's probably a life-form from another galaxy. She likes making children unhappy. She lives off —

That is quite enough!

Miss Stoney looked very stern. "There's a big difference between being concerned about the other children and making unpleasant and silly accusations. I would prefer to see you older ones trying to be extra helpful to Mrs T during this settling-in period. I think you'd better go now. I will be keeping an eye on things."

"I knew she wouldn't believe us," I said when we got outside. "I should have explained it better."

"It wasn't your fault. I don't think she would have believed us anyway," said Stacey.

At dinner-time that day, I had a horrible feeling that Mrs T knew exactly what I'd been thinking about her. She began to act differently towards me.

First, she made me sit away from Josie. Josie didn't seem to mind. I could hear her going on to Kelly about what fancy dress they were going to wear at the youth club that night.

Then she told me off for pushing when we went to get our coats. When I said I hadn't been pushing, she said:

Well dear, we're being just a teeny-weeny bit rude, aren't we? I think we'd better go and see Miss Stoney until we calm down.

Miss Stoney made me miss dinner-play. I didn't care. I didn't want to be out there anyway. I could see Josie chatting to Kelly.

Josie sat with Kelly in class. I was on my own by the window. I didn't feel like working. I felt awful. I wanted everything back to normal, to be how it was before Mrs T had come. I'd been happy then. Josie and I had always been friends and now… It was all Mrs T's fault. She'd done it. I wished she'd disappear off the face of the earth – for ever.

Chapter Seven
Help at Last

I walked home on my own after school.
My mum wasn't there when I got in –
nobody was. I got a biscuit and sat on the
step outside. I didn't eat it, but began to
break it into little bits.

It was Jamie's mum from next door.

I shrugged.

> Hello Jessica. Are you all right?

> Isn't your mum back yet? Come in with me and have a drink. Jamie's watching TV.

I followed her in, and she asked me, "What's the matter?"

I broke down. The words came tumbling out. I couldn't have told my own mum. She always thought I exaggerated and made things up. But Jamie's mum was different, she really seemed to listen. I told her about Mrs T and what she'd done to Jamie and how she was splitting up Josie and me. I told her about the flash of light that was Mrs T beaming down, and how Miss Stoney had got cross when Stacey and I had tried to tell her.

"Why wouldn't she believe us? Do you think I'm making it all up?" I was close to tears by now.

Jamie's mum was quiet for a long time and then she said:

No, I don't think you're making it up. I think something is very wrong.

But why, why don't the teachers see what's going on? And stop her?

I don't think teachers always understand what's happening. They don't always see everything — not all the little things. Sometimes they're just too busy or tired.

But someone's got to stop her. She's making everyone unhappy. Couldn't you speak to Miss Stoney?

Jamie's mum shook her head. "I don't know what I could tell her unless I'd seen Mrs T making children unhappy myself. I can hardly go into school and watch her."

Couldn't you go to the youth club?

She nodded slowly. "I suppose I could go early to fetch Jamie. There should be more adults there anyway to look after so many children. I don't like the thought of him being there at all, but he wants to go again because Darren is going."

"I'm only going because Stacey asked me. Stacey's mum says she's got to go. Neither of us really want to."

Stacey and I went to the youth club that night. Most people, including Josie and Kelly, were in fancy dress. We wore jeans.

It was horribly hot. All the doors and windows were closed and Mrs T was playing very loud music. It was quite dark and there were flashing lights. Everyone was tearing around, screaming and shouting and getting really excited. Darren hit his head jumping off a table. Kelly had sprained her ankle and was sitting on the floor crying. People were tripping over her.

Mrs T seemed to be glowing. Her hair was swaying wildly with the music. Her skin looked tight and shiny. She was grinning like mad and dancing around. She didn't seem to notice the children getting hurt.

She spun round
faster and faster,
wobbling from
side to side.

come on everybody

like this!

Come on. Keep moving!

She
seemed
to be getting
bigger by the minute.
It was disgusting to watch.
No one was enjoying it any more,
but Mrs T kept on at everyone. I saw
her grab Jamie and try to spin him
round, but he pulled away from her.

Suddenly, she caught sight of me and
Stacey standing by the door.

Come on you two, everyone's got to join in!

NO! We're not at school, We don't have to.

We shook our heads. She stared at me; her eyes seemed to be going right through me. I stared back. I knew I mustn't let her win.

She gave me a look that seemed to will me to sink through the floor…But the moment passed and she swept by with the music. I felt Stacey squeeze my hand. "She doesn't like you."

I know.

I felt quite brave, but sick and shaky at the same time. I began to pray that Jamie's mum would turn up soon – before anything *really* awful happened.

55

I watched Mrs T weaving her way towards Jamie. She knew he wasn't big enough or old enough to stand up to her. I saw her take hold of him. She was trying to get the other children to help her drag him into the middle of the floor. Jamie's shirt was tearing. He was crying and kicking, trying to break free of her grasp.

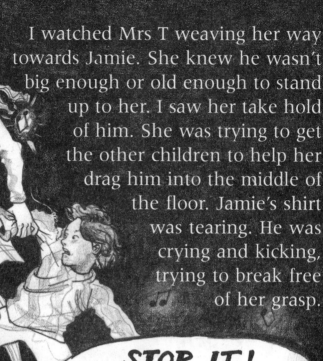

STOP IT!
He doesn't want to dance. Leave him alone. you HORRID PERSON!

I heard my own voice screaming above the music. I could hardly believe it was me.

The hall went deathly quiet. The music had stopped. Everyone was standing very still. Mrs T slowly let go of Jamie and turned to face me.

"Well, well, and who have we here? Miss spoil-sport, know-it-all Jessica Brown," she hissed. "How dare you! How dare you speak to me like that!"

She was walking towards me, her face red and bulging as if she were going to explode.

YOU STUPID STUPID CHILD! What right have you to interfere? How DARE you spoil everything! You nasty, tale-telling, little girl!

LEAVE HER ALONE!

She was coming closer and closer. Her eyes were like tiny black points. I could hear some of the little ones crying.

The main lights flicked on.

I think that's enough for one evening!

Jamie's mum
must have seen
and heard everything.
She spoke very slowly
and calmly.

Mrs T seemed to crumble.
She stood there swaying, very flustered –
not knowing what to do. Then at last she
smiled, her horrible, sickening smile.

I could see Jamie's mum looking quietly at the pale, tear-stained faces of the children and their torn costumes. Jamie ran to her. Darren was clutching his head and moaning.

Mrs T gave Jamie's mum a knowing look.

"I think we'd better all sit down and play I-spy until our mummies and daddies arrive," she added, quickly trying to gather the children round her. But everyone just stood quietly by the door, waiting for their parents to come.

59

Chapter Eight
Beamed Back Up?

The next day Darren and Kelly were off school. Josie sat next to me but didn't say much. In fact everyone was very quiet.

Just before dinner-time we saw Jamie's mum come into school with two other mothers. They were in Miss Stoney's office for a long time.

It was a strange dinner-time. Mrs T didn't
speak to any of us as she dished out the
food. And when we went outside, she
stood on her own at one end of the
playground. She looked very thin.
Her hair was like straw and
her tights were sagging
and wrinkled.

We all got on with playing,
enjoying ourselves like we used to.
The little ones were messing about with
bits of chalk. Some of us were playing
football. Mrs T gazed round the playground – she seemed to be trying to sniff
out some misery – as if she desperately
needed a whiff of it to keep her going.
Only, none of us were miserable.

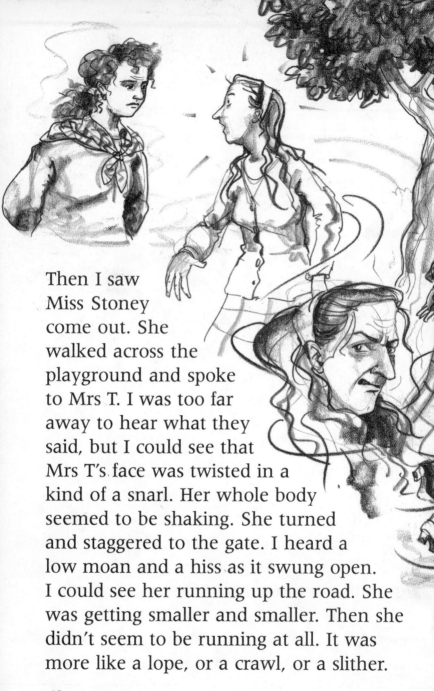

Then I saw Miss Stoney come out. She walked across the playground and spoke to Mrs T. I was too far away to hear what they said, but I could see that Mrs T's face was twisted in a kind of a snarl. Her whole body seemed to be shaking. She turned and staggered to the gate. I heard a low moan and a hiss as it swung open. I could see her running up the road. She was getting smaller and smaller. Then she didn't seem to be running at all. It was more like a lope, or a crawl, or a slither.

Mrs T was slithering away into the distance.

We never saw Mrs T again. No one spoke
to us about her. Stacey said that because
it was all hushed up, it proved Mrs T was
an alien. We never knew whether Mrs T
had beamed back up or just gone to make
people miserable somewhere else. At
least she wouldn't be coming back to us.

There were only two days of term left and
Miss Stoney and Miss Swan had to look
after us during their dinner break. After
the holiday we got a new dinner lady –
Mr Jones. He was great. You could tell he
really liked children.

We went round to Mrs T's old house once, to see where she had lived. The lady next door told us Mrs T left one day and never come back. "Funny woman – kept herself to herself. We asked her round for a meal once but she wouldn't come!"

We peered through the window. In one corner, there was a pile of old clothes and shoes. And something else – something crumpled.

Anyway that's what Stacey and I thought, and Stacey's my best friend now.